GIVE THE DOG A BONE

STEVEN KELLOGG

SEASTAR BOOKS

New York

Boppity BAM!
For Arlen and Sam.
Nickity NACK!
For Peter and Zack.

Copyright © 2000 by Steven Kellogg

SEASTAR BOOKS
a division of NORTH-SOUTH BOOKS, INC.

First published in the United States by SeaStar Books, a division of North-South Books, Inc., New York.
Published simultaneously in Great Britain, Canada, Australia, and New Zealand by North-South Books,
an imprint of Nord-Süd Verlag AG, Gossau Zürich, Switzerland.

Library of Congress Cataloging-in-Publication Data is available.
A CIP catalogue record for this book is available from The British Library.

The art for this book was prepared using a combination of colored ink, watercolor, acrylic, and colored pencil.
The text for this book is set in Kennerly, Windsor, and Bostonian.
Designed by Judythe Sieck

ISBN 1-58717-001-9 (trade binding)
3 5 7 9 TB 10 8 6 4 2
ISBN 1-58717-002-7 (library binding)
3 5 7 9 LB 10 8 6 4 2

Printed in Hong Kong

For more information about our books, and the authors and artists who create them,
visit our web site: www.northsouth.com

This old man, he played ONE,
He played nick-nack on his drum.

Nickity Nackity
Nackity Nickity
Nickity Nackity
Nackity Nickity
Nickity
Nackity
NACK!

Nick-nack paddywhack, give the dog a bone,
This old man went rolling home.

This old man went cobbling home.

This old man, he played FOUR,
Nick-KNOCK, Nick-KNOCK on the door.
KNOCK-nack, paddywhack...

Would you like a BONE?

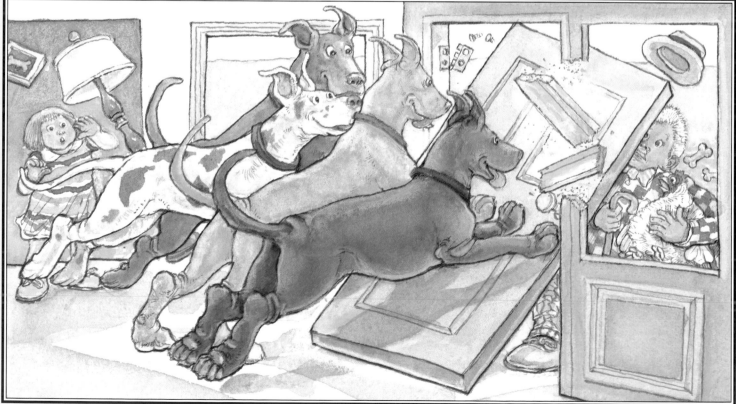

This old man was welcomed home.

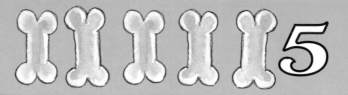

Toss the dogs a bone,

This old man hightailed it home.

This old man, he played SIX,
Told the hen to hatch six chicks...

Nick-nack paddywhack, took the chickies home,

Nick-nack paddywhack,

Eight kind sled dogs hauled him home.

This old man, he played NINE,
Playing nick-nack, feeling fine.

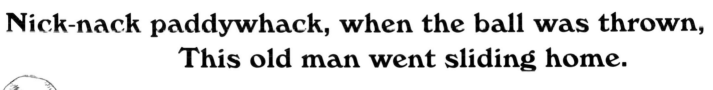

Nick-nack paddywhack, when the ball was thrown,
This old man went sliding home.

Nick-nack, shells crack,

29

Raptors want a bone...

Grabbed their bones and raptored home.

 **A NOTE ABOUT THE SONG**

This Old Man is a popular nonsense counting song of uncertain origin (perhaps English, perhaps American) that seems to have first appeared in the early twenti-eth century. Hundreds of variations can be found, since improvisation is often the most entertaining part of any singing game; this version takes off in an entirely original direction after the first verse. Some accompaniments include clapping, stomping, drumming, and motions such as tapping the shoe (for *on my shoe*) or revolving one arm around the other (for *rolling home*). As memorable as it is amusing, portions of this song have been used in joke-telling, pop music, and in the study of speech development. It teaches language, counting, rhythm, and coordination. So . . . *nick-nack paddywack, sing the song below!*

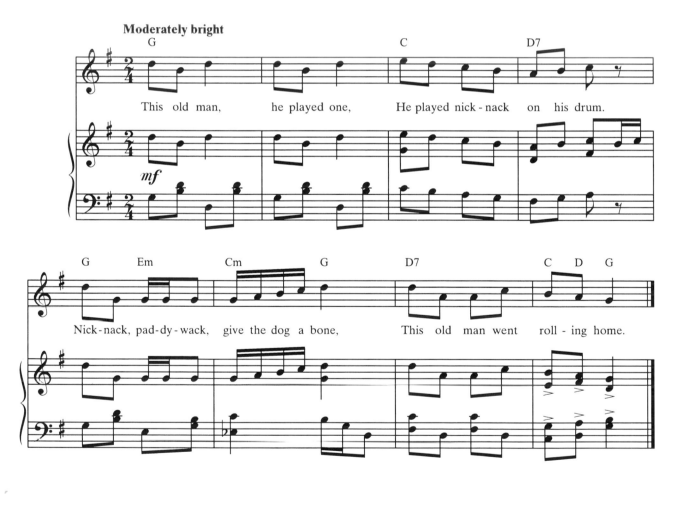